Y0-DNM-056

For Ron,
We hope
you enjoy the
stories.

Best regards,

Janet Rhodes
Michael Rhodes

TALES OF THE LIVING ROOM WARRIOR

by Janet Rhodes

Illustrations by Michael Rhodes

Also by Janet Rhodes

Fiction
Chocolate and Cabernet (2009)
https://www.createspace.com/3388474

Copyright ©2009 by Janet Rhodes

Cover design and illustrations ©2009 by Michael Rhodes
All rights reserved.
No part of this book may be reproduced in any form without permission in writing by the author, except by a reviewer who may quote brief passages in a review.

This book is dedicated to Rascal, an intrepid spirit who ruled our living room for seventeen and a half years. We are sure that she is now clawing a couch somewhere at the end of the cosmos.

Acknowledgments

We would like to acknowledge the following people, without whom this book would be a lesser work:

Joan Morrow, who read the rough draft many years ago and encouraged Janet to keep going with the fables.

Dr. Josie Thompson & the entire staff of the Civic Feline Clinic (www.civicfelineclinic.com) for the compassion and kindness they showed Rascal and her humans.

And the anonymous ladies who put out food for the tuxedo cats at the Walnut Creek Bridge.

A Note to Our Readers

This eight-part fable is intended for every lover of cats, books, fantasy, fairytales, folktales, science fiction, and whimsy' and for anyone who desires a brief vacation from the cares of being a grown-up. May these tales give you moments of delight and provoke a smile that lingers for days.

Tales of the Living Room Warrior

A Fable in Eight Parts

Prologue

EVERY person privileged enough to share her home with a cat knows what the ancient Egyptians knew. He knows what the Huichol tribe of South America, the Parsees, Celts, Scandinavians, Finns, and Chinese Buddhists also knew. No cat, not even the most diminutive house cat, is entirely ordinary.

Few people today appreciate the true origins of cats, associating them as we do with a comfy spot on the living room sofa, a sunny window sill, or a rug near the fireplace. After centuries in our homes, much wildness still clings to cats. A flash of bird wing by your patio door, and your sleepy companion steps into the role of predator, reminding you that he is a cousin of the jaguar and the cougar. Each paw is picked up and placed down with fluid precision as he races lightning-quick toward the glass.

On even the most mundane day, your living room warrior may hone his skills at stalking and hiding. He disappears for inordinate periods of time, for the cat's body is so loose it can be poured like cake batter into any shape its feline owner desires. Thus an aura of mystery surrounds every cat.

But when a cat looks at you, she moves beyond the mysterious or the wild. She re-establishes the feline reputation for magic. For the cat is doing more than just looking. She is studying you, examining you, indeed, taking you apart to reach your soul. And as she does so, she is guided by that singular light which illuminates feline eyes.

Perhaps she is also recalling the early days of cats, aeons before they conquered the human hearth. Indeed, in its earliest days, heaven was an exclusively feline establishment although humans with any knowledge of this are vanishingly rare. None of us would recognize the heaven of so many aeons ago, and certainly not earth, because the world as we know it today did not yet exist. Our planet was actually a rubber ball in a nondescript shade of gray, lolling about on a cloudbank. In short, the world was then a cat toy.

In those early days, neither heaven nor earth possessed any colors. Every drop of color in the universe still belonged to the sun. The celestial felines did not look like cats on earth today. There were no calicoes or tabbies or tortoise-shells, for every one of those coats requires at least a spot or a sprinkling of color. Nor did those early felines have the green, blue, or amber eyes with which we are now so familiar. Instead, the eyes of those first cats were clear orbs sparkling with curiosity.

Although a few lucky cats were black as night or white as snow, most were a somewhat   dusty shade of gray. Indeed, there was a great deal of gray among those early felines due to their celestial residence and its proximity to the sun. Every morning, as the sun rose, the cats drew toward it. They crept or inched or scampered across cloudbanks until all clustered along a fringe of cloud as close as possible to the rising sun. Then every single feline would settle down for the day, some on their backs, others on their sides, but every single belly was poking out of the clouds toward the sun.

One of those cats was named Alice. Like every cat in heaven, Alice was initially only black, completely black from her nose to the tip of her tail. Due to her inordinate love of the sun's warmth, Alice's fur had been bleached white in some places. She wore four white booties and a white bib which began at the base of her chin and narrowed as it ran down her throat. Although she had mere dashes of white on her back and sides, a big spot of white splashed across her belly.

Although Alice savored the warmth of the sun like every single celestial feline, she differed from the others in one regard. She coveted not only the warmth of the sun, but his colors as well. But for her steadfastness, we would still have no colors today.

The sun briefly shared his colors twice each day, but then slowly withdrew them, leaving behind only a pale blue stain on the sky every morning. But in the evening, the sun did not leave even that. The sun withdrew every scrap and spot and drop of color and took all these back into himself, leaving nothing behind but blackness, a blackness so intense it was not interrupted by even a pinpoint of light.

Fortunately, the cats could see in the dark. Few celestial felines troubled themselves over colors. When the sun rose each morning, the cats reveled in the toasty warmth of the clouds, seeking out the best place – the cloud most likely to keep its golden warmth throughout the day. To other felines, the colors bleeding from the sun whenever it rose or set, the shafts of sunlight teasing through the clouds in the most improbable places — these were merely a pleasing backdrop, as soft music is to dinner with candle light.

For every resident of heaven accepted without question that felines were entitled to divine treatment. No one ever questioned whether heaven was rightfully theirs, or whom the colors belonged to. The antics and surprises provided by the sun and his ability to radically change colors whenever he rose or set were merely a diversion, a brief source of entertainment heaven was required by some unseen proprietor to provide to its first residents to modulate their experience of bliss. Otherwise, even bliss could become monotonous.

Alice, however, longed for colors. She didn't just want to see colors. She wanted to have some colors that were her own, that belonged to her — and no one else. She wanted to wear colors. Alice even longed for a big pot of colors she could use whenever and however she wanted to. The luminous colors of the sun drew her toward them like a magnet. Alice did not decide to steal colors from the sun. Rather, she simply could not help herself.

To Alice, the ever-changing light of the sun became a source of fascination. She pursued it the way a feline today will chase the red dot of a laser pointer. Alice was just as determined to catch it, pounce on it, and claim ownership. She chased after the light in the sky as if it were a living thing.

Every day began as a light spot of gray appeared on the eastern edge of heaven. Slowly this gray spot grew and spread across the sky, pushing away the inky blackness of the previous night. Blackness gave way at its edges to deep purples and midnight blues, as if the night were sluggish somehow and not quite sure it wanted to leave. But just like the cats, the night sky could not resist the warmth and power of the sun.

The sun worked hard every morning as he steadily pushed the night away.

The sun possessed enormous heat and power. Indeed, had he not allowed his colors to escape and spread across the sky, the sun might have exploded. Just as water will bubble until it rolls over the top of a pot left burning on the stove, so would the sun boil over every morning.

The first colors out of the sun's cauldron were those of fire — red, orange, and yellow. Pink and lavender followed. Lime green snuck out after them and elbowed its way in here and there among the clouds. Soon the sky became so crowded with colors that they bumped against each other. Red would move across a cloudbank, pushing orange and yellow out of its way. Eventually orange would dribble off the clouds and leave scattered puddles of tangerine. And yellow was stubborn.

After most colors had left heaven and returned to somewhere behind the sun, yellow remained. It covered the face of the sun. Sometimes yellow hung on the clouds until late in the day. On those days, anyone who looked up could believe a goldsmith toiled in heaven, hammering thin metal ribbons to the edges of clouds.

That was yellow asserting its rightful place. And Alice was as stubborn as yellow. On one particular morning the sun outdid himself. And so did Alice.

The sun spilled so much red that as he withdrew, he stained the cloudbanks pink. While everyone else napped, Alice set to work. First she stepped with determination into a cloudbank and stood still for a very long time up to the tops of her white booties in all of that pink. Then Alice stepped out with a look of accomplishment on her face. She immediately looked down. She was nearly overcome with disappointment. Her booties remained as snow-white as before.

Next she crouched down low and stretched her chin out to rub her white throat against the pink clouds. But Alice did not know whether it had worked. She soon realized she had no way of seeing her own throat. So she decided to try something else. She plopped down on her side and rolled around in the pink clouds, rubbing her white belly against them just the way a cat will roll about in a pile of torn wrapping papers and discarded ribbons left after a birthday party. Although the clouds were silent and did not make those delightful crunching paper noises, they yielded the same results.

When Alice rolled on her back and craned her neck to look down at her belly, it remained just as white as before. Still, Alice would not give up. She hunkered down and studied the clouds. Presently, she came up with another idea — the same idea that will eventually occur to every cat who plays too long with party leftovers.

She knew it would take some time but that the colors would return before nightfall. She remained alert, hunkered down on her cloudbank and waited for sunset. That evening as the sun released his colors, Alice started to eat them, first a lemony swatch of cloud, then smatterings and droplets of tangerine, lime and blueberry, followed by ribbons of red licorice. Alice felt the warm colors filling up her belly. But these did not satisfy her.

The sun had left enormous areas of cloudbank stained the same lovely shade of pink as that morning. These beguiled Alice. She had to have them. She crouched low on all four paws. She ate fast and with utter concentration, de- vouring one pink cloudbank and then another and another, just like someone eating cotton candy in an amusement park.

But Alice did not stop. She was in such a hurry to purloin as many colors as she could, she did not notice how heavy her belly felt, or how low it was drag- ging in the cloudbank. Finally a low gurgling noise emitted from her belly. She had to stop. She remained hunkered down and grew very still. There were so many more colors and she did not have much time before nightfall. But Alice could not eat any more, not even one more tiny meringue-like wisp of cloud.

Although she had stopped eating, her stomach seemed to be doubling in size. The gurgling in her belly grew louder and turned into a low rumble that started at the base of her throat. It traveled upward. Alice remained crouched and still. There was nothing else she could do.

Soon her sides started to heave. Poor Alice began to regurgitate. She simply could not help herself. As she barfed up the evening's brilliant sunset, colors flew everywhere. Indeed, there was chaos. For a long time after Alice's mis-adventure, every cat in heaven as well as the contents of the celestial kitchen, pantry, and party closet looked like a tie-dyed tee shirt. It took quite a while for this riot of colors to sort itself out. Eventually it was deemed proper that most rubber balls should be red, most cardboard boxes a dull brown or gray while a select few containers could sport many colors as did kites and ribbons and wrapping paper.

And as for the felines themselves, most opted for dignified coats in subdued hues. But no one was able to escape from Alice's colors. Even the most snow-white cats have blue eyes. And even the most purely black felines have amber or green.

To this day, no one knows why the sun never tried to reclaim the stolen colors. Perhaps there was some distaste. But Alice's misfortune is our great fortune. Thanks to her misadventure, we do not have to even consider what the world would be like without colors.

The world was created by a cat named Chester. This cat was up in heaven, as all cats were initially. He had been looking for the warmest, sunniest spot to lie down and take an afternoon nap. There was an infinite supply of such spots, so it became difficult to choose.

Chester was looking for something new. He forgot all about his nap and began investigating heaven's supply of cat toys. Among these were red rubber balls. So, this bored feline took to batting a ball around heaven, dodging in and out among the cloudbanks, getting more and more reckless until he batted that ball so hard that he knocked it right out of heaven. It fell miles below the clouds. It landed so far from the sun it began to turn blue and green.

The sudden change in temperature and the shock of its fall transformed the ball's composition until it retained only a wee bit of rubber. It had become mainly earth and stone and water.

Meanwhile, Chester became deeply chagrined, as would any cat who has just lost his favorite toy. He kept hanging out of heaven and swinging at that lost ball, trying to retrieve it and bring it home. Most of the time he missed and we should be grateful that he did. For, every time he batted the earth, his paw caused an earthquake. Mountains were formed, glaciers began to slide southward from the North Pole, leaving lakes and oceans behind.

One day, Chester sat on the precipice of heaven, he had become that confident in his exquisite balance and superb muscular coordination. No doubt, you have seen cats do this on second and third floor window sills. So determined was he to catch his favorite toy that he batted away at the earth fiercely, so fiercely, in fact, that he was hanging upside down and didn' t notice that he was losing his balance because he almost had the world between his front paws. He tumbled and fell out of heaven and kept on tumbling until he landed somewhere on the great plains of Africa.

When Chester landed, he hit the earth with so much force that it started spinning and has never stopped.

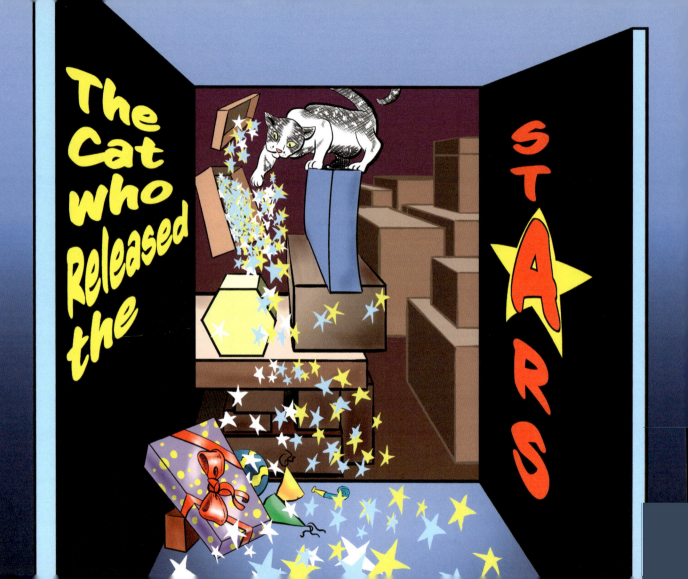

The stars were initially just confetti. However, they were very special sparkling silver-white confetti which was stored in a cardboard box high up on a shelf in a storage closet in heaven. This whole closet was full of party supplies, and the door was kept most of the way closed.

It was never completely closed, because cats cannot manage very well with door knobs. So the door was left ajar and pushed open whenever streamers or confetti or funny paper hats were needed. Contrary to common belief, heaven was not one long, uninterrupted celebration. Although the occupants of heaven were in a continual state of bliss, they tried to observe some days as ordinary and mark others as cause for celebration.

One day a cat named Fred squeezed through the small opening between the door and the door jamb and went into the closet not to retrieve supplies, but just to explore, for no cat worth its toy mouse will leave any closet unexplored for long. Anyone who has witnessed such explorations will not be surprised to learn that Christopher Columbus got the idea to discover America from watching his cat examine the contents of the wardrobe. A feline inventory of the contents of a closet is no mere exercise in curiosity. If you have witnessed your cat's seriousness of purpose on a closet expedition, you have no doubt realized that he is rubbing himself against your shoes to exorcise their demons. Likewise, your best wool suits, favorite shirts... for anything worth doing is worth doing thoroughly.

In fact, to leave any corner of a closet unexamined would amount to a dereliction of feline duty, for every cat worthy of being killed by curiosity knows that the lost continent of Atlantis is in someone's bedroom closet or dresser drawer and is determined not to overlook it. The cat who was exploring the party closet up in heaven was no exception. Fred rubbed and peered into every party hat, stepped on every paper horn and crawled into every box he could fit into, for this particular cat was portly and less than graceful.

Still, that did not deter him from climbing up on the closet shelf to continue his tour. In the midst of his perambulation, Fred knocked a plain cardboard box off the shelf. It fell open as it hit the floor. Instantly, a thick luminous carpet of confetti spread across the bottom of the closet.

Up in heaven, all rooms were as porous as colanders because they were essentially made out of clouds. So, as Fred was making his way down to the closet floor to gather up the sparkling confetti, a wind suddenly arose and blew every last bit of it out of paw's reach. The confetti was scattered far and wide across every inch of heaven. When we look up at night, we can still see it and we call it stars.

The Cat Who Shaped the Constellations

A FTER the wind stopped, the night sky resembled dotted Swiss, for the confetti was spread more or less evenly across heaven. Initially, there were no constellations. These were created by a most unusual cat named Tabitha. Her contribution was twofold, for although she invented the constellations entirely by accident, she made the moon with painstaking care.

Tabitha's father was a pumpkin-colored tabby and her mother was a longhair whose sumptuous fur was almost entirely snow-white. When humans see the latter type of cat, we often say that it must be part angora because the fur is so long, thick, and luxurious. Tabitha resembled both of her parents. Like her mother's fur, most of Tabitha's was pure white and exceptionally luscious. She bore her father's pumpkin tabby markings on her back and on the top of her head, but these looked frosty and soft compared to the markings of most tabbies, as if their tiger stripes were drawn with pen and ink while Tabitha's were done with a watercolor brush. The big splash of color on her back was most orange at its center and became more frosty as it spread out until it melted into the surrounding whiteness. The gradation of Tabitha's markings was as subtle as the blush on a peach.

Maintaining such an impeccable appearance was hard, but Tabitha's fur coat never had a smudge, for she took inordinate pride in her looks. Tabitha decided that the stars were going to waste. Remember that these stars were sparkling white confetti with just a hint of silver. They were pleasing to Tabitha's discriminating eye. Although she always groomed herself until her coat shined, it had never sparkled. She realized that she could use this confetti like dusting powder and make herself shimmer.

But first she had to collect it and that was no easy task, as anyone who has ever tried to scoop up spilled confetti knows. It is even more difficult if you do not have hands. Tabitha faced an exceptionally difficult task.

She strolled into the storage closet and began looking for a suitable container.

Tabitha looked at the plain cardboard box that had initially held all the confetti, for it was still lying on the floor. Fred, the cat who had knocked it off the closet shelf was so embarrassed that he rushed off in a hurry, or in as much of a hurry as his portly frame would allow, leaving the box on the floor and the closet door wide open.

Tabitha did not waste much time considering that box. She quickly flicked her right front paw in a gesture of disdain, then delicately lifted her chin and pointed her pretty pink nose up in the air as if to say, how common. Such a crude container would be entirely unsuitable for her dressing table.

She scoured the closet floor but still found nothing she could use, for even though the boxes were filled with wonderful things like brilliantly colored paper streamers, the boxes themselves were plain. Some were square. Others were rectangular. Some were wide and flat like dress boxes. Others were as deep as barrels. But they were all drab brown or dull gray. None were pretty.

Tabitha climbed to the top of a tall narrow box and vaulted from it to the closet shelf. Immediately, she could see that the boxes up there were much better suited to her needs, for they were smaller and more colorful. Aside from half a dozen rather pedestrian shoe boxes, a Monopoly game, and a Scrabble board, all of these boxes were cheerful. There were four jigsaw puzzles whose boxes were adorned, one with a woodland scene, another with tropical fish, and so on.

But Tabitha pushed past these, for at the far end of the shelf, she saw a number of ladies' hat boxes. Now these looked smart. Most were octagonal and pastel-colored. Some were solid. Others were adorned with flowers. But one box stood out. It was perfectly round and was silver both inside and out. Tabitha could see inside, because the lid was made of clear, rigid plastic. She stood on the very edge of the closet shelf and peered down right through the lid. The box's silver lining dazzled her. This was the most simple one of all, but its elegance appealed to Tabitha.

There was no question about it, this box was the cat's meow. Getting it down from the closet shelf without scuffing its gleaming silver shell would be no easy matter. But Tabitha persevered. She gently nudged it off the shelf onto a very tall box, then down from there onto a slightly shorter box until eventually she had her silver box down on the floor of the closet. It sustained only a few slight scuffs.

Tabitha got behind her box and by butting it with her head, began to push it out of the closet. Soon the sun went down and the stars came out. Tabitha wasted no time. She knocked the lid off her box with one swipe, then turned it on its side and began rolling it with her left front paw while she pushed stars into it with her right. Anyone who has witnessed a cat playing with its favorite toy will realize that Tabitha worked with absolute concentration.

She began to use her new powder immediately and liked its effect. The first night, she completely emptied the box when she powdered herself. She peered into the silver lining as she tried to paw out the last bit of powder and saw her own reflection gleaming back at her. Tabitha liked what she saw.

She gathered stars on many nights for it requires infinite patience to scoop up even a small amount of confetti, especially when you have only paws to work with. As Tabitha worked, she began to notice a short-haired tabby named Euphrates. One night she glanced up and noticed that Euphrates was watching her with more than casual interest. He was a light gray with deep charcoal gray and black markings of which he was infinitely proud. His tiger stripes were as bold and definite as Tabitha's were soft.

Euphrates's eyelids slid down slowly until his eyes were nearly closed, but it seemed to Tabitha that he was watching her even more intently now than before. His nose began to quiver very slightly and he raised his chin as if he were inhaling the air around Tabitha. She noticed that his throat and chest were not gray at all but were the color of sand. His eyes were the same warm color.

From that moment on, Tabitha thought of nothing else, not even her silver hat box filled with luminous confetti. As far as she was concerned, Euphrates was the cat's pajamas.

Tabitha fell in love and not just with any cat, for Euphrates was the lead feline of heaven. He was a most prepossessing fellow, and he knew it — unfortunately, as it would turn out for Tabitha. One day, she became so smitten that her love overcame her natural reserve and she decided to give him her most prized possession — her big round silver hat box filled with as much confetti as her paws could scoop up.

In fact, Tabitha worked so hard at scooping up as much confetti as she possibly could (and it was very uncharacteristic of Tabitha to work hard at anything unrelated to grooming) that she thoroughly cleaned up the sky. After the sun sank, heaven became completely black for the first time that anyone could remember since the closet mishap.

Tabitha slid the clear plastic lid across the top of her silver box, then climbed up on top and let her weight drop until she heard the lid snap tightly closed, for she was determined to lose not a single star. She was standing on the biggest cloud of all right in the center of heaven.

Euphrates lay on his side at the far end of it. His body was completely limp and seemed to melt into the cloudbank. But his neck was erect and his head was raised in an attitude of watchfulness. Anyone who has seen a lion resting will recognize this posture and the supreme confidence it expresses.

Tabitha proudly began to push her treasure across the cloud. Euphrates watched her as did all of the cats in heaven, for everyone was gathered there. Cats who were entirely black mingled with cats who were black but wore white bibs and booties. Calicoes and tabbies, some brown, others gray, a few pumpkin, all mingled on the cloud. There were spotted cats and Manx cats, Persians and angoras. All watched Tabitha.

Most watched in silence. A few heartily approved of Tabitha's mission while others demurred. And a very select few felt apprehension, for they knew that Euphrates was proud not only of his markings but of his tabbiness itself. Unbeknownst to Tabitha, he took such infinite pride in his purity that he disdained the company of most other cats.

Finally, she had pushed her gift all the way across the cloudbank until she stopped right in front of Euphrates. Then she sat down with the perfect composure of a lady who is wearing white gloves. She watched Euphrates with eager anticipation. But he did not move.

Seconds passed. There were no clocks in heaven then, but everyone recognized the passage of time because they felt the cloudbank shift and roll a little.

Euphrates was not acknowledging the gift, and he was not even acknowledging Tabitha's presence. At first, she could not believe it. She thought he must not understand. So she reached out from where she was still sitting and nudged the gift forward a little with her right front paw.

A low rumbling came from Euphrates's throat. There was no mistaking it, he was angry with Tabitha and wanted her to leave. Still, Tabitha did not move.

Euphrates's paw shot out like lightning and knocked the round silver box on its side.

Tabitha was beside herself. The cloudbank was still crowded with cats, and she felt deeply humiliated. She never looked at Euphrates again, nor did she glance at any other feline. She needed a solitary place to regain her composure. So she stepped off the cloudbank and wandered across the newly blackened spaces of heaven. She walked with no particular purpose, but absentmindedly as dejected lovers often do.

Unbeknownst to Tabitha, a great deal of sparkling white confetti was clinging to the pads of her paws and left marks in the sky wherever she walked. Her first steps into the blackness were the brightest ones. These are Venus and the North Star.

But Tabitha left many other marks as well. We call them Orion, the Big Dipper and the Little Dipper. For awhile she paced back and forth, mindlessly shedding much confetti from her paws. She left a big powdery white swath in the sky, otherwise known as the Milky Way. Whenever the night is clear, we can look up and see Tabitha's footprints.

We can also see the gift that Euphrates rejected, for his angry swipe knocked the round silver box on its side. The luminous white confetti is plainly visible through its lid, for this is the moon. Whenever the moon is very bright and viewed from a certain angle, we can still see the scuff marks Tabitha made by knocking it down from the closet shelf.

Some people might be glad that Tabitha selected a box whose sides were perfectly round while others may regret her choice and wish that she had chosen an octagonal box, for it is that perfect roundness that forces the moon to roll endlessly around the dome of heaven. Had Tabitha chosen an octagon, perhaps the moon could rest.

The Underbelly of Heaven

MEANWHILE, Chester, the feline who landed on earth, was beginning to realize that he deeply missed the company of other cats. Throughout the day, he would gaze heavenward and study the clouds. He quickly noticed how different each cloud was from its neighbors and how much they all changed. Some clouds were like feather quills; they spanned the blue dome separating earth from heaven. Others formed big snowbanks whose shadings changed from gray to white. Still others looked like wisps of smoke.

Sometimes the clouds appeared motionless. On other days they drifted lazily. And at other times, they raced across the sky, scurrying just the way the cats in heaven did when they were playing a game.

Slowly Chester realized the clouds were out of his reach. No matter how far he stretched, he could not touch them. He could touch only the shadows they cast on earth, although he did not think of this place as earth, Indeed, he had no name for this strange new place where he was trapped. There must be a way home, Chester reasoned. He just had to find it.

Although Chester filled his days by chasing clouds and pouncing on their shadows, his nights were long and empty. During this period, the stars were still confined to the inside of a plain cardboard box up on a shelf in heaven's party closet. At night, the sky became as black as ink. The whole world turned so black there was not one pinpoint of light anywhere. Night after night, Chester would lie on his side, curl himself up into the tightest ball he possibly could, and wrap his tail over his eyes while he tried to forget where he was. As he lay perfectly still, his mind gamboled about heaven. His memories basked in warm, gentle weather. Soon he was darting through sunlit clouds as he indulged in parties and games with other cats.

But no matter how diligently he worked at remembering heaven, the cold damp earth he bedded down on always reminded Chester of where he was. Although he did not know the word, gravity, Chester knew that something was pinning him down here. He felt as if he had been swallowed up by some huge force and was stuck inside it like an undigested mouse.

Chester regarded the world in much the same way a writer looks at a blank sheet of paper, as merely a surface to catch the words that come tumbling out. The world's grassy plains and sandy deserts were nothing more to Chester than a broad, empty surface whose only purpose was to reflect the shadows of passing clouds.

One evening, Chester became so afraid of the coming night he turned his back on the setting sun. He could no longer bear to watch that burning sphere sink below the rim of the world. Nor could he force himself to witness the soft stain of many colors it would leave behind. Instead he gazed eastward at the pool of indigo spreading rapidly between himself and heaven.

Chester's eyes suddenly widened for something new rose above the horizon. It was big and round. And it was white, kind of a silvery white. It shone. Light spilled from it down to earth. This round glowing ball was like the sun, but it was clearly not the sun. While the light of the sun was so fierce one could not look straight up at it, this light was soft. Then many tiny marks, each one a mere pinprick of light, appeared one after another throughout the sky, just as if someone up in heaven were drawing a picture.

Surely the cats in heaven were sending him a message. He could not decipher it, but its lovely light filled Chester with joy. He was no longer alone. Night after night, he gazed at those silvery white marks as milky white light from the new round sphere spilled down on him. He wondered what they meant.

All of these new lights had appeared so suddenly they must mean something special. Chester pondered the soft white globe and the many new marks criss-crossing the night sky in much the same way a person would study an old letter written with a fountain pen in a beautiful flowing hand, especially if its words belonged to an unknown language and the soft yellow paper bore the scent of something vaguely unfamiliar. Chester treasured those new marks in the night sky exactly as a person would save such an uncommon letter, uncertain of its meaning but determined to find out.

One day, late in the afternoon, the light changed rapidly. Feathery clouds began to race across the sky and tumble over themselves. The air soon smelled wet and heavy. New clouds arrived in every shade of gray. The clouds themselves, not just the sky, but the clouds themselves, began to turn black. There was no sunset. A wind pushed up the fur on Chester's coat, and he trembled, not just from the cold but because he knew that something new was happening.

Suddenly great big drops of water pelted Chester. The dirt around him turned to mud and sucked at his feet. Sheets of water poured down from the sky, flattened the grass around him, ripped flowers from their stems, and smashed delicate petals into the ground.

Still, Chester would not run or hide from the storm for he was determined to find those silvery lights in the black sky. He looked heavenward even though drops of water pelted his face. There was no sunset. It suddenly became night, and nothing appeared in the sky. Nothing at all. This alarmed Chester.

What if all this water washed away the messages the cats were sending him? Surely, those marks in the sky were intended for him to decipher and when he did, he would know how to get home. What if he lost those messages? He would be trapped here forever.

Chester stood vigil all night. He never took his eyes off heaven, or rather, where he was certain heaven must be, because he could see nothing at all. Even the deepest layer of Chester's brown coat became soaked. Icy water ran down inside his ears. He was forced repeatedly to close his eyes. The ground sucked at his white boots, which were now filthy.

Finally, morning came and the rain stopped. As the sun rose, Chester suddenly understood the meaning of all those marks left night after night in the sky. Or, at least he believed wholeheartedly he had deciphered those messages the cats were sending him. Of course, they had been telling him they were building a bridge to connect heaven and earth. Chester now stood under it, a seven-colored bridge which started at one end of the earth, rose in a perfect arc, and spanned the entire sky until it reached the opposite end.

Chester marveled at it. The bridge had seven stripes: red, orange, yellow, green, blue, indigo, and violet. A plain steel gray span would have been enough. The cats had really outdone themselves, how hard they must have worked and how sorely they must miss him to have constructed this bridge whose colors glowed and melted into each other like softening ice cream.

Chester wasted no time. He bolted toward the farthest end of the world to find that bridge as fast as he could. No matter how hard he ran, the edge of the bridge moved too. It was always a little ahead of him. It maddened Chester, for he badly wanted to get back to heaven.

But then he realized that although the bottom of the colored bridge always moved away from him, the rest of the arc remained still. Chester reasoned that if he could just find a really high spot to stand on, he might be able to reach up and stretch high enough above the earth to catch the lower part of that arc.

So, Chester stopped and looked around. He took off at full speed for what we now call Mt. Everest. His size was prodigious, for in heaven there had been no reason to stint on the cats' proportions.

Chester vaulted to the top and used that mountain peak just as a person might use the kitchen stool to reach up and grab a favorite teapot placed atop the kitchen cupboard. He stretched upward like a rubber band pulled so taut it is ready to snap. And it worked! His left front paw brushed the lower end of that bridge. He sunk his claws into the indigo and violet bands. He batted away with his right front paw until its claws also gripped the bridge. At first, his lower torso and hind legs swung out wildly above the earth. But Chester clung desperately to the violet and indigo bands with all of his front claws and used every balancing trick a cat knows to heave himself onto that bridge.

And he did it! He was standing on the arc, all four feet planted firmly on the topmost band of color, the red one. He was on his way home. Chester nearly burst with anticipation. He gazed up at heaven as he walked. The white cloud-banks were rimmed with gold.

Chester did not even glance down at earth, which is most unfortunate. Had he looked down, he might have noticed the seven-colored bridge was beginning to bow under his weight. The prodigious size that had enabled him to bound across the world, spring to the top of Mount Everest, and stretch across the sky – that same size would now be his undoing.

As Chester ran toward the top of its arc, the seven-colored bridge sagged deeper and deeper. Suddenly, Chester was tumbling through the air and pieces of the bridge were falling around him. Cats and party favors tumbled through the sky alongside him. The cats howled. He knew their names: Eugenia, Maximilian, Jack, Sassy Boy, Enigma...

Cats and party favors pelted earth. A pumpkin shattered so forcefully it split Africa in two. The broken piece skidded southeast across the Indian Ocean until it stopped at the South Pole, where it stayed and eventually became Antarctica.

A paper horn rolled across North America and whistled a bit halfheartedly as it did so. While party favors lay scattered on the ground, the cats quickly righted themselves and screeched at Chester. "What do you think you were doing?!"

"Coming home."

"You just ripped a hole in the floor of heaven! And half of heaven is pouring through it!"

"But what about the bridge?"

"What bridge?!" All of the other cats shrieked in unison.

"What about the notes you were writing in the sky?"

"What notes?!" the cats demanded.

"That big silvery white ball and those pinpricks of light in the night-"

"Hah! Confetti! Nothing more than spilled confetti," snorted an orange cat with black stripes who contemptuously turned his back and trotted across the world to what is now called India. Indeed, the cats were so angry with Chester and the rude way he had spoiled heaven that few of them stuck around. They scattered to the far corners of the world.

Chester was as disappointed as someone who has treasured a fragile letter, held its dusty paper between his fingertips and wondered over its origins until he has it translated and discovers it is nothing more than a grocery list. Perhaps worse, Chester's loneliness was now wedded to a deep sense of embarrassment. He felt like someone who believes he has been invited to a party as its guest of honor, only to step through the doorway and be met by a roomful of cold stares. Chester wandered until he stumbled upon a cave in which he secluded himself for a very long time, as he needed solitude while he recovered. Indeed, Chester was mortified by the hole he had unwittingly ripped in heaven's under-belly. So deep was his chagrin that he eschewed the sunlight for the remainder of his days, emerging from his cave to hunt only at night. And to this very day, his many descendants are nocturnal creatures.

HEAVEN careened about like a piñata struck by blindfolded children. Clouds pitched up and down and sideways in wild attempts to regain their equilibrium as cats hissed and yowled their displeasure. Thousands of claws sunk deep into the clouds. Many feline tails disappeared entirely from view, tucked between legs and under bellies. But many other tails were all too visible as they whipped back and forth.

The door to heaven's party closet swung open. Storage barrels tipped over and rolled about, thumping against each other. Boxes fell off the top shelf and broke open. Paper streamers and ribbons tangled themselves around party hats. Christmas ornaments sparkled in every color imaginable as they became rolled up in the mess along with orange and brown paper turkeys and stern cardboard pilgrims.

Euphrates raced along a cloudbank, leaped over the hole in heaven's floor, and pushed his way into the party closet. He scoured its contents, looking for something to patch the hole before more of heaven's residents could fall through it and crash to earth. But the overturned barrels and hastily emptied boxes revealed nothing more suitable for patchwork than several rolls of tape. Some were masking tape, and others were scotch tape — intended only for hanging streamers and wrapping presents.

Clearly these would never do. Heaven's emergency required something much sturdier. Euphrates stood stock still and peered intently at the closet's cloudy floor. Easter bunnies lay on their sides. Pink, yellow, and blue eggs rolled about, bumping into bright red hearts and shiny green shamrocks. Euphrates's dismay deepened as he looked around. But he was following only where his eyes led him.

Meanwhile, another feline embarked on a different route. A somewhat portly black and white spotted fellow aptly nicknamed Fat Cat, remained still but alert, sunk deep into the middle of his cloud. Fat Cat slowly stretched his neck up and leaned his head back. Soon his nose started to quiver, but not with fear.

He stood up, placed each foot with purpose and discretion, and slowly advanced across heaven toward the kitchen. His generous belly brushed the cloudbank, and his nose quivered more and more as he followed the scents wafting out. For while the party closet had unleashed a riotous tangle of shapes and colors; in heaven's kitchen, bowls of whipped cream tipped over, milk spilled, pounds of butter plopped off countertops and landed on toasty warm clouds. But to surpass all of these blended aromas, from somewhere — a fridge door had been knocked open or plates had been overturned — and not one or two or three, but hundreds of thickly sliced bacon strips had landed beside the butter on those same toasty clouds. Heaven's kitchen was sizzling and smoking and smelling, well, heavenly.

As Fat Cat moved toward it; Euphrates, Madge, Tip, and a rather fastidious Siamese named Madeleine followed. All were determined to repair heaven and set things right. Unfortunately for heaven, Fat Cat, and Tip would soon be tempted away from their mission. But in heaven everything had a way of turning out right. So, perhaps it was no mere coincidence that Madeleine was so fastidious, even for a cat.

While Tip, a black cat, buried his nose in a pile of whipped cream; Fat Cat explored the toasty warm cloud below heaven's longest kitchen counter. He was, no doubt, determined to test the suitability of bacon grease and melting butter as patching materials. And toward that end, Fat Cat, strolled slowly, picking up as much butter and bacon as his paw pads and generous furry belly could absorb.

But Madeleine paused and looked about her at the overturned dishes, pots, pans, and cutlery. Copper cookware flashed rosy warm in the sunlight. Stainless steel spoons and spatulas glared brightly. The kitchen's cloudy floor was covered with food, and many different types of foodstuffs were beginning to mingle with each other. Although they smelled wonderful right now, soon these would become somewhat less than appealing.

Meanwhile, the contents of the party closet were rolling all over heaven. Some slid into the kitchen. A small Santa Claus on a sled came to a stop in the midst of it all.

Heaven was a mess. Madeleine lifted her head and slid her eyes halfway closed when she spotted something that nearly undid her. It was most unfortunate that when Chester had started homeward on the rainbow bridge, his paws were exceedingly muddy. Not only had he broken the rainbow and ripped a hole in heaven, but he had also left big, dirty paw-prints all over the blue sky. No celestial feline had ever seen mud before; they did not even know the name for it. Madeleine peered at the offending paw-prints with dismay. They were most unbecoming. This would not do.

Although she did not know exactly how to get rid of the mud, Madeleine knew that hot water was good for cleaning things. She was not sure how she knew it, she just did. So many things in heaven were like that.

So, Madeleine walked over to the big white enamel stove in the middle of heaven's kitchen. She stood up on her hind legs and reached up with her long, elegantly black-tipped paws. Placing one paw against the oven door, she batted away at a stove knob with the other. She swatted at the stove knob repeatedly until it finally turned with a decisive click. A long hiss followed as a blue flame sprang up under the cast iron burner.

Madeleine immediately turned her back on the stove and set to work on her next task — finding water and a pot to heat it in. She strolled into heaven's pantry and looked about. In an instant, the copper pots caught her eye. They had such a warm, rosy hue and sparkled beautifully — even the tiny gold screws securing their polished brass handles. She selected a deep soup pot from the lowest shelf of the pantry and knocked it off with a few deft swipes of her paw, then butted it with her head through the pantry door.

As Madeleine emerged from the pantry, Euphrates was standing in the middle of the kitchen and looking all around him. He watched her move her twinkling soup pot across the kitchen's cloudy floor with a series of head butts. He noticed that various foodstuffs were beginning to mingle with each other as they rolled and trickled across heaven's kitchen. And he noticed with extreme displeasure that Tip and Fat Cat had immersed themselves in whipped cream and bacon fat.

Euphrates emitted a low, rumbling growl of displeasure. No one but Madge noticed. He jumped up on a long butcher block counter that ran right down the middle of heaven's kitchen. As he paced the length of the countertop, Euphrates's every movement from the placement of each paw to the tilting of his head and the half-closure of his eyelids evinced his utter disdain for his fellow felines and the ease with which they had slipped into distractions. Muddy paw-prints did not matter now. Neither did feasting on whipped cream and bacon, for this was heaven and pleasure would always be available as long as heaven remained intact.

He watched with growing dismay as Madeleine attempted to lift her pot up to heaven's stovetop. She looked about her and tried to catch his eye, but Euphrates looked away. He would not assist in such a colossal waste of time and effort. He abruptly flicked a paw in her direction to signal his displeasure and turned his head away, glancing up toward the cloud hovering above heaven's kitchen. A light warm mist was thickening into steam over heaven's stove. Chester's paw-prints began to soften and drip slowly toward earth. But this did not interest Euphrates.

He looked instead at the door to heaven's pantry, which was ajar. Euphrates knew that everything was liquid or soft — whipped cream, melting butter, bacon fat, and droplets of steam condensing from the overheated clouds. But still the hole in heaven's floor gaped wide open. The melting butter, bacon fat, droplets of steam and whipped cream just dripped through it in one continuous stream and landed somewhere below, probably on earth.

This would not do. By now, Euphrates was thoroughly disgusted that Tip, Fat Cat, and Madeleine were entirely ignoring his rumbled warnings. He turned his head toward Madge and stared at her intently. Then he jumped off the counter and took a few steps across the cloud stretching toward the pantry door. He paused and looked back over his shoulder. Madge was following. She was a somewhat dusty gray-brown cat with thick fur, a round flat face, and a pudgy body. She was not someone Euphrates would have chosen as a companion, but she alone of all the cats in heaven's kitchen was acknowledging his authority.

He strolled through the door to heaven's pantry without looking back again. He was confident that Madge was following him. Euphrates sat down on the cloudy floor and looked up. As he surveyed rows of pots, jars of pasta from spaghetti to bow-tie and corkscrew-shaped rotini, he saw item after item that would not do. He was sure that every bit of pasta, every measuring spoon, flowered tea cup, or matching saucer would just fall through the gaping hole in heaven's floor and plummet to earth.

But finally his eye caught something that intrigued him. While everything in the pantry enticed his eye with colors, unusual shapes, decorations, or polished surfaces; this one item was dull — so dull that Euphrates had initially overlooked it. It was a huge burlap sack lying on the floor of the pantry. The sack was dull brown and had no shape to speak of, but if they could just drag it and push it across the hole in heaven's floor, maybe it would be sufficient.

Euphrates got behind one corner and butted it with his head. Madge got behind the other. She butted it too. As they crouched and pushed and butted away at the heavy sack, their tails swished back and forth. Many culinary items lined the lowest shelf of the pantry. A few were knocked over. A white teacup with purple violets was knocked sideways against a skillet by a wayward swipe of Euphrates's tail. It shattered with a brittle sound, but no one paid it any mind. The task Euphrates and Madge focused on was too important. The saucer was a bit more fortunate. It tipped and fell sideways through open slats in the shelf. It landed safely and soundlessly on the pantry's cloudy floor.

As they shoved the sack through the narrow opening in the pantry door, Madge and Euphrates crouched over it in utter concentration, the muscles in their shoulders and haunches tensed and stood out, sharply defined under their fur. Both tales swished energetically and more pantry items met their demise. Eggs broke and lay in pools on the pantry floor until yolks and whites dripped through the clouds at varying rates of speed. A plate of drying herbs slipped off the shelf and through the pantry's porous floor. Soon, the scent of rosemary drifted across heaven. And as they made one final shove through the doorway, two small cylinder-shaped cardboard containers also fell, swept off the shelf by their tails. As they rolled about, they spewed salt and baking powder. But no one paid any mind because these were white and fit in nicely with the cloudy backdrop, unlike Chester's offending paw-prints.

As they began to inch across the kitchen, Euphrates trotted around to the front of the sack and took a corner of it between his teeth. He pulled hard. But it was unduly heavy and hurt his mouth. Steam from the overheated clouds was now filling the kitchen, enveloping both Euphrates and Madge. This annoyed Euphrates. He let out a low, long mew to signal his displeasure. Once again, he was ignored by everyone but Madge. And Euphrates was not used to being ignored. Even among cats, his presence usually commanded attention.

But Madeleine never even glanced over her shoulder. Her back remained turned toward Euphrates while she stood on her hind legs and swiped ineffectually at the remaining smudges of Chester's now running and dribbling muddy paw-prints. She clicked her tongue in frustration. Euphrates looked around him. Tip and Fat Cat were still on the cloudbank below, each one engrossed in the task of meticulously cleaning whipped cream and bacon fat from his coat.

Heaven was still pitching and rolling about, although a little less frantically than before. But most cats still clung, eyes wide, yowling, and tails whipping. This was taking too long. Euphrates spun around and hooked one of his front paws into the burlap. If he dragged it, this would be faster. He swiped hard at it to get his claws anchored in.

The burlap split wide open, and white flour poured out. It coated Euphrates and Madge, sprayed across the kitchen, dusting Madeleine and the stovetop. But most important, the flour landed. And as it landed, it bonded with the condensation dripping from the overheated clouds. The flour landed in the whipped cream, which was thinning and beginning to run. And the flour landed in the melting butter and the bacon grease — and, yes, on Fat Cat and Tip

57

too.

And as the flour bonded to all of these, the stove continued to heat up heaven — until the celestial felines inhaled something new and wonderful. Indeed, no one in heaven had ever seen or smelled or tasted a dumpling before. But suddenly dumplings were everywhere, plumping themselves up and sliding about all over heaven, just the way they will float in a bowl of chicken soup.

As the dumplings floated and skated about, heaven regained its equilibrium. Although the clouds had always moved continually, these movements had balanced each other like the pieces of a mobile — until Chester's actions had sent it into a seesaw. But the dumplings were setting everything right. Indeed, they patched the hole in heaven's floor so nicely that no celestial feline has fallen through it ever since, although we do sometimes claim it's raining cats and dogs.

Incidentally, as the steam from Madeleine's stove gradually cleansed Chester's muddy paw-prints from the sky, this too helped to set heaven right. For mud does not belong in heaven. If heaven is to retain its magic, its luster, mud must remain on earth. Although Euphrates disdained Madeleine's obsession, her contribution was greater than anyone could have imagined. She helped to restore the sense of balance the universe depends on with all things being in their proper place.

However, Madeleine's diligence did produce one unintended consequence. As the stove remained on for an inordinately long time, it heated up the clouds and it heated up heaven to such high degrees that the universe expanded. Heaven grew and grew. The earth below also swelled in size. The distance between heaven and earth grew even more.

The cats alone remained the same size. So where they once loomed large, they were now quite diminutive. But to this day, no cat has ever forgotten his true proportions. And anyone who has made the acquaintance of a single feline can attest that every cat everywhere retains the memory of his original place and is aware of the true size of his footprint upon the world.

ƞє night fog touched the earth for the first time. Fireworks were also invented. Today few people know that both occurred on the same evening. Although humans had been on earth for millennia, the cats in heaven were unaware of them. Indeed, heaven and earth had traveled so far apart the cats had never noticed the hundreds of fires early humans built to warm themselves and cook.

After all, if you are walking with a friend and he strikes a match, of course you will notice it. But suppose someone is walking five blocks ahead of you on a dark city street. If he strikes a match, you would not see even the tiniest pinprick of light. Well, neither did the cats in heaven. But that would change on this particular evening.

Such is human nature, or at least the nature of some humans, that the need to just fool around overpowers every urge of caution or common sense. Why, the person who created fireworks is not unlike a cat who keeps running inside a paper grocery bag just to hear it rattle. One night this fellow simply had to combine gunpowder with fire just to see what would happen.

As he tinkered unseen, miles below heaven, cats gathered on the biggest cloudbank right in the middle of their celestial home. The inky sky revealed no more than the thinnest sliver of a crescent moon. A slender, small-boned feline rubbed herself against a catnip toy. She was so black she would have melted into the sky surrounding her had it not been for the light gold dusting across her fur. This was the closest thing she had to markings, for she possessed neither white bib nor booties. But the moonlight picked out this gold dust and because of it, the others called her Feldspar.

Meanwhile, a calico zigzagged after a cat dancer. This same toy provoked the curiosity of a gray who was so determined to catch it that he executed a triple back flip and landed on his two hind feet. He stood nearly straight up for several seconds as he batted frantically with both front paws but still managed to catch neither the long springy wire nor the the scraps of paper attached to the end of it.

Tabbies, spotted cats, angoras, Siamese, and felines of every description jumped about, ran, tumbled, and rolled through the clouds. Still, heaven remained quiet even though it pulsed with feline energy. Cat feet make little noise, especially when they land on clouds.

Suddenly all acrobatics stopped. Everyone's ears turned sideways. The night whined just as if an enormous insect had left the earth and was flying up in a long arc toward heaven.

Boom! The clouds vibrated. So many sparks of yellow and orange filled the sky it seemed as if an enormous round flower had burst open right below them. The flower hovered for a moment and gave off a smoky scent until its millions of fiery petals melted silently into the night.

The cats peered down. No one noticed that the moon had been knocked over. Behind them, it lay on its side like a delicate evening bag that has been tossed on a chair and neglected.

No one tut-tutted that their peaceful evening had been rudely interrupted.

Nor did anyone hiss. All of the cats peered down through the clouds and crouched forward with such concentration their muscles stood out like ropes.

Soon the noise was heard again. This boom was followed by a long green arc that shot across the sky before it fell apart. Millions of tiny red sparks followed the next boom. These opened slowly like one big umbrella before falling softly and quietly back to earth. A bright white flower was next. Its petals shot out in all directions like long spears before curling up and inward.

For a long time, no one moved. Not the slightest hint of a meow, purr, or any feline noise whatsoever was heard. No cat could take her eyes off the world.

This was completely new, there were no words for it. Indeed this was so new there were no emotions which seemed proper to express. Should they feel annoyance or joy? Who or what had taken the night sky and used it as his personal canvas?

Heaven became drugged by curiosity. This was not lightning. Nor was it a shooting star. Was it an angel or demon who painted these pictures with fire?

Whichever it was, the fire painter was down on the earth below the cats. That was the only thing they could tell for certain. But that only made the fire paintings more freakish. Light belonged in heaven. The world received only as much light as heaven could not use. The sun was the only source of fire and light the cats had ever known. No cat could think of anything nearly as powerful as the sun. But even the sun could not do this.

The cats felt more than a desire to know. As they peered down through the clouds, every feline in heaven became overpowered by the need to know what was going on below them. Had the world sprouted arms and legs, and begun turning cartwheels, it could not have surprised the cats any more than it already had.

After all, while heaven lay in darkness, the world spat fire. What could be more strange than that?

Throughout these nocturnal explosions, the cats had been as still and quiet as statues. The world had so mesmerized them that they lost all awareness of themselves. The cats listened with absolute concentration until they discerned that one spot would pop and sputter after every fire painting. They had become more aware of this tiny spot on the earth, miles below, than they were of their own feet.

Before anyone realized that he had lifted a paw, all of the cats raced across heaven. Clouds were dislodged and scattered as they poured across the sky. Heaven tilted to one side. It was entirely one thing to all gather and frolic on the central cloudbank, but to all run abruptly to the farthest outcropping of cloud at the edge of heaven, well, that was another matter. Heaven is not unlike a rowboat, for it depends upon its occupants to to help it maintain its equilibrium.

No one hesitated as they neared the edge of heaven. In one moment, they reached the outermost cloud, which was very small and poked out of the side of heaven just the way a tiny, jagged point of land juts out into the surrounding ocean. Only, this cloud had no secure underpinning. In the same moment, everyone leaned forward and looked down just as if they were peering over the edge of a cliff.

Heaven moved unsteadily beneath their feet. But no one noticed until heaven pitched forward suddenly and began rolling over on one side like a rowboat that has lost its balance and is about to turn over in a lake.

Cats were being shaken about as heaven pitched and rolled. Many were nearly tossed out of heaven like dimes and nickels falling out of a pocket. Every cat sunk his claws into heaven. As heaven tilted even more sharply, clouds began avalanching downhill toward the cats. Pretty soon, heaven was falling. The cats hung on. Heaven fell fast. It was dropping like a stone. It seemed that nothing would break its fall until it smacked right into the earth. Heaven was not intended for such use. What would become of it?

The cats felt a violent impact. Snow exploded in their faces and covered their fur. They had just sheared off the top of a mountain and left a funny-shaped, blunt-end cone behind them. Still, heaven kept falling.

A mountain range stood straight up from the earth like a row of enormous stone teeth. The cats plummeted toward it. Suddenly heaven stopped. Everyone felt as if they were being pulled backward like a rubber band. One cusp of the moon had gotten caught on the mountain peak. The moonlit end of heaven tilted up while the rest of heaven dangled down loosely, nearly brushing the earth.

The jarring motion made fur stand up. Every cloud rumbled and shook as heaven finally came to a stop. While heaven trembled, the cats inhaled smoke.

They began to smell gun powder, roast duck, and ginger. Subtler aromas such as green tea and steamed rice also made their presence known.

The cats peered down. What they now saw below enthralled them even more than the fire paintings had. A crowd of strange furless creatures who were clearly not cats filled a city square. The cats recognized them as people because of their resemblance to some of the toys in heaven. However, the toys were tiny and inanimate. These creatures were huge, bigger than the cats themselves, and much louder. They did not stop chattering, even for a moment.

What was more, the people were brighter than birds. They wore jackets and pants in every color imaginable. A woman in a long, plum-colored dress strolled just beneath the cats. A flowering branch meandered across her back and spilled over her right shoulder. A brown bird sat in the fork of that branch, almost in the middle of her back. A pale pink blossom rested on her collarbone as a yellow butterfly hovered just below it.

The cats were amazed. These people not only made pictures on the night sky, but they carried pictures on themselves. The woman shimmered as she walked. In fact, so did everyone else. The cats did not yet know it, but they were hovering over China. The people's clothes sparkled and shone as they did, because they were woven from silk thread. Some clothes, like the plum-clad lady's, were richly embroidered. But even the simplest, unadorned clothes caught the fire's light and reflected it like water.

Up in heaven, the cats preferred pastels and muted hues. Although they could festoon heaven with the brightest colors whenever they chose to empty the party closet, the cats seldom did. Their senses had always been coddled, for the sights, smells, sounds, and temperature of their celestial home were calibrated to induce bliss. A riot of colors, smells, motion, and noise now assaulted them.

Some cats were delighted. But, quite frankly, others were horrified.

Presently, the cats saw the fire painter, a tall, thin man whose head was nearly bald. He had a closely trimmed beard and was dressed very simply, all in black silk. He stood a small distance away from the crowd and a little above them, for he was on a knoll. He alone was quiet, for he seemed to be concentrating fiercely on what he was doing.

While the cats watched, the heat of many cooking fires melted the snow they had gotten on their fur. Beads of cold water ran down their haunches. A drop landed on the head of the fire painter. Suddenly he stopped what he was doing, put his hand on his head, and looked up with a startled expression.

A sense of foreboding filled the cats. He was staring right at them. They did not know if they should mingle with these new creatures. It might be better if no one knew they were there.

But, as the fire painter looked up, his gaze was unfocused. He could not perceive the shapes of the cats through the gray blur of heaven's floor. Soon, others looked up as drops of melting snow landed on their heads. But they all stared in the same way. No one seemed to be able to see the cats.

Still, others in the crowd felt no drops of water. But everyone soon felt heaven's cool breath. Some crossed their arms and hunched down inside their clothes. A few grabbed the front collars of their jackets and pulled them forward, as if protecting the backs of their necks. People began to leave the square and go indoors.

The fire painter shivered a little as he gathered up his toys. This chagrined the cats. But there was nothing they could do about it. They had ended up here by accident and no one knew how to get home.

Soon the square was empty. The fire went out. The people took the roast duck indoors with them. The night became silent, dark, and cold. Every cat realized that they were now marooned in this desolate place.

They hunkered down and waited for something to change, for something to happen that might enable them to go home. There were thousands of cats in heaven and a great deal of snow still lay on their fur. The felines drizzled lightly on the town square throughout the night. As the last drop of melting snow hit the earth, a faint, rosy gray spot appeared at the bottom edge of the eastern sky. This spot began to spread. A little yellow ran into it, just as if someone was melting butter.

Soon the cats realized that the sun was rising. Everyone was glad to see it, but only because it made them less miserable. They still did not know how to get home.

Meanwhile the sun kept pouring itself out on the world. The sky turned slowly from gray to blue. The sun was becoming too bright to look at. The cats squinted and turned away. They were beginning to feel less cold. Then a strange thing happened. While the felines looked down at the town square, it became smaller. Soon they realized that heaven was rising. The sun had warmed up the clouds. They began to swell and spread out.

The cats could feel themselves floating upward. They believed that they needed to do nothing except sit still as heaven became more buoyant. It would be just like riding in a hot air balloon.

Suddenly heaven was jarred. The cats felt themselves being pulled sharply backward. Then the motion stopped and heaven slowly rose again, but only a few inches before it was yanked back down.

Most cats had fallen asleep by now. They opened their eyes and looked around blearily. The few cats who had remained awake were of a rather nervous nature. One of these spread himself on his belly and yowled. Another began clawing away at her cloud, treating heaven no better than a living room sofa.

Meanwhile the sun continued to lift heaven upward while something else kept yanking heaven down. After several minutes of this, the cats began to hear an ominous sound, just like a sheet being torn in two, but this sound was much heavier.

If anyone in the world had looked up right then, she might have seen something that looked like a dusty black velvet ribbon rippling through the clouds. Feldspar alone realized that if heaven was ever going to return home, someone needed to unfasten the moon. The moon was sliding back and forth across that giant tooth of a mountain peak. Whenever heaven moved, the mountain would release one cusp of the crescent moon. But almost immediately, the other cusp would get caught.

Feldspar raced across heaven. She was faster than a shadow and seemed just as insubstantial. As soon as she reached the mountain peak, she crouched low, leaning precariously off her cloud, and caught the moon with her teeth. Feldspar jerked her head up and the moon was freed. Nothing impeded heaven's progress now. The rest of the cats' journey was uneventful and they were soon home.

Eventually their cold, desolate night of being stranded was forgotten and they remembered only the delightful parts of their adventure, which compelled them to visit the world often. From time to time, they laid eyes on earthbound cats — those felines who had been rudely knocked out of heaven by Chester's misadventure. The sight of cats on earth so enthralled celestial felines that they would lean most precariously out of heaven. But try as they might, the celestial felines could not reach their earthly brethren. And in this one respect, the world's cats were just like its humans — they could not see through the floor of heaven. When they looked up, they saw only a gray blur.

Incidentally the world had no plateaus before that evening. These were created by heaven's cats. Now there are many plateaus on every continent of the world, evidence not only that celestial felines have visited the world often, but also that their urgent curiosity has caused them to be a bit reckless in piloting heaven.

The First Living Room Warrior

Most warriors conquer by brute force. But the truly skillful insinuate themselves into coveted places. Thus did earthbound cats secure for themselves their new territory — the human household. To a wolf, the human hearth is invulnerable. To a cat, however, it is like the city of Troy.

One of the cats who had been rudely ejected from heaven was a clever fellow named Albert. While Chester and many others slunk off into caves and withdrew into a multitude of hiding places, Albert immediately began to investigate this strange new place.

He soon discovered that he liked the forests, for they teemed with rabbits, mice, and birds. From the moment Albert stepped under the trees, he forgot the world's wide open places. The plains had been blasted by winds and relentless storms. The desert sand was hot and the sun burned his eyes. Too many of the mountains were made of inhospitable rock. But the forests grew in deep loam. And this was covered by decaying pine needles and leaves.

For the first time since leaving heaven, Albert stood on something soft. Accustomed as he was to strolling across cloudbanks, most surfaces of the world were harsh. The pads of his paws had become so hard, dry, and cracked they bled when he walked. Albert moved slowly, one step at a time. The floor of the forest moved gently beneath him. Nothing would ever caress his feet as gently as the clouds had. Nevertheless, the forest would do.

Cool, thick shadows allowed him to open his eyes wide. Albert looked long and hard. He crouched low among ferns and studied the floor of the forest. A light brown spot scurried through the leaves and vanished under the root of a tree. It moved so fast, it was a blur.

Then a bigger creature with long ears hopped about, rustling leaves wherever it landed. Albert remained still and close to the ground while he watched it. He noticed how its nose quivered whenever it stopped. Soon, it smelled him and took off in a lightning burst of speed, its white tail streaking through the forest like a comet.

Albert didn't follow. He was much too weary to hunt. Besides he didn't know how. It had never been necessary to hunt in heaven. Although the cats played at chasing toys and one another, they had never hunted, for food was plentiful. But Albert's hunger would quickly teach him to hunt. Soon, he would become sleek from the mice and rabbits he would catch. Eventually, he would catch birds too, although these were more difficult.

However, the sight of birds did not amaze Albert, for he had frequently seen them in heaven. He and his fellow felines would crouch low on their clouds to look down at them. Now, he had to look up. Whenever a wing flashed bright yellow or a scarlet throat appeared above him, Albert raced back and forth, crashing into thickets. Finally he realized they needed to land. He used these opportunities wisely.

On his first day in the forest, he heard a new sound. It was unlike anything he had ever heard in heaven. Curiosity drove him toward it. He inched forward until he saw a long ribbon of water tumbling and rolling through the trees. The water turned frothy white and bubbled up wherever it pounded over rocks.

Elsewhere it was clear, then blue and silver all at once. Sunlight bounced off it.

Albert crept toward it. The river never stopped moving, but it didn' t run away from him the way the strange new creatures had. He lowered his head and drank long and slow. The water was cold. It tasted as exquisite as anything he' d drunk in heaven.

Soft mud oozed between the pads of Albert's front paws. It soothed him. The velvety wetness slid into the cuts on his feet. And wherever it moved, the pain went away. Albert turned sideways to the river. He let his hind paws sink into the brown-black stuff. Now, Albert had always been fastidious. It was not like him to go lolling about in mud. But this felt delicious.

Albert's eyelids slid down. His chin pointed upward, baring his long throat to a shaft of sunlight that reached gently through the trees. He had nearly abandoned himself to bliss when the forest changed. Crackle! Crunch! Something was moving toward him on heavy feet. Albert's eyes flew open. He was alarmed. He tried to spring uphill, but the riverbank sucked at his feet. This new creature was big, much bigger than the ones that had scurried away from him.

Albert studied the trees. He spotted something white poking out behind the leaves. This puzzled him. The creature drew closer. More bones fanned out in a lacy pattern, but they were hard, so hard they pushed the leaves aside. Albert couldn' t run. He sank down as low as he could without getting his belly in the mud. His haunches stood out. Every hair of his short gray-blue fur stood straight up. Albert struggled to remain still, but his whole body quivered. He was feeling something he had never felt before — fear.

The creature emerged from the leaves. Albert was amazed, for it carried enormous and intricate horns on a small head. The animal looked straight at Albert, but its large brown eyes were docile. It then ignored Albert, headed straight for the water, lowered its head, and drank. Others would come to the river that day. Many times, Albert witnessed this. The ribbon of water drew every creature toward it.

The big ones drank from the river. Those who were very small drank from puddles in the forest floor, for the river was powerful and might carry them away. Albert would spend days crouched in the underbrush near these water holes as he taught himself to catch mice and songbirds.

The forest soon became as familiar to Albert as every nook and cranny in the cloudbanks of heaven had once been. Those strange white horns no longer startled him, for they were merely the antlers of deer. And deer are not hunters. Albert feared no creature except the wolf. That was the only creature in the forest who could hunt him.

Or, so Albert believed.

He was not troubled by the thin plume of gray smoke that curled upward through the forest every evening. It rose above the crowns of the trees, then melted into the sky. Every night, the smoke appeared in the same place. As the sky blackened and the creatures of the forest became quiet, the smoke disappeared. The next day the smoke would appear again, and always at the same time, just as late afternoon was yielding to the night. Then the smoke would disappear at the same time, in the dead of night when the whole forest was asleep.

On his first night in the forest, Albert had smelled the smoke. He had watched it every night since. But he was not curious about it, for he had become a hunter. And as a hunter, he could see no use whatever for smoke.

The forest was pleasant. The nights did not get too cold. Although it rained often, Albert knew many places where he could shelter. But Albert did not know that this was summer. He had not been on earth long enough to experience a change of seasons. One night when he curled up in his den, the ground felt cold, colder than the night before. Albert grew impatient for the night to end. The next morning, the sun was sluggish. It rose later than usual. And the sun appeared weak. Its light was more gray than gold.

Mice and rabbits began burrowing deeper into their holes. They came out seldom. The days were now as cold as the nights had once been. Leaves began to change. Albert had always been somewhat indifferent to colors. Although the forest possessed infinite shades of green from the palest lichen to the deepest fern, he had never concerned himself with it. But green was now disappearing from the forest.

Albert crouched near his favorite water hole and waited a long time. A bright spot of yellow fluttered in the thicket ahead of him. He sprung forward. But when he stared down at the yellow pinned under his feet, it was nothing but a leaf, nearly as thin as a butterfly's wing.

Soon all of the leaves were turning rust, brown, yellow, and scarlet red. Albert looked up in the trees; they were ablaze with colors. This disgusted him. How could he spot a bird in that splotchy mess? Birds no longer landed at the water holes. The forest grew more quiet each day. There was no birdsong now.

Albert trotted along the riverbank and trained his eye along the tree roots. Surely, a rabbit or a mouse would have to emerge. The river sounded louder than it ever had before, although it was not swollen with rain. Rather, the forest around it had grown quiet, and the thick greenery that used to muffle the river's noises was steadily thinning. Albert could look right through undergrowth that used to conceal animals and there was nothing there.

His paws hit the ground silently as he ran. Albert heard only the river and the sound of his own breathing until something barked high above him. He looked up at the dull sky and saw a black spot moving just below heaven. More black specks and scattered barking noises followed it. The barks were thin, but they were growing. Soon the barks were as loud as a pack of dogs, and the whole sky was cut in two by an enormous black triangle flying straight as an arrow.

Albert knew what this was. He had seen geese in heaven. But looking down at them from the comfort of a cloudbank, he' d had no idea that autumn was occurring on the world below him and this was driving the geese south.

Albert looked up and studied them. They never broke formation. There was a sense of urgency to their flight. Albert ran after them. Of course, he couldn' t catch them, and he knew it. No earthbound cat could jump that high, for the geese nearly scraped the bottom of heaven. But sooner or later, every bird has to land.

Albert streaked along the riverbank. He ran so hard he panted until his tongue hung out, but he didn' t stop or slow down. Geese are big, powerful birds that can cover miles before resting. Albert ran until his sides ached, his heart pounded, and his mouth got so dry it hurt. But still he kept on.

The sound of his panting was so loud he could barely hear the river. And that must be why Albert didn' t realize that someone was now running behind him. Albert ran due south. The plume of smoke was behind Albert for it was in the north. And it was from this direction that the stranger had come. Like Albert, he had seen the sky split by the wedge of geese. And, like Albert, the stranger was a hunter of consummate skill.

The flock began to dip like the head of an arrow shot toward earth, first the point and then the masses of geese filling out the wedge. The sky grew blacker and louder with the beating of their wings.

The river bent westward, but both Albert and the stranger ran straight ahead. A flat silver-gray spot was spreading out ahead of them, like a mirror laid down on the ground. The grass became tall, and the ground grew mucky. Tall thin rods stood straight out of the water, and big brown lumps of fuzz covered their tops. These looked odd to Albert. But the stranger knew they were cattails. He began to crouch down and walk in a low stance, allowing the cattails and the tall grass to conceal him.

As the geese landed, the surface of the marsh exploded into a billion droplets of water. These flashed silver-white like new stars before falling back down into the duller water of the marsh. The geese began to drink. Long necks which had been held so straight during flight now curved gently as they dipped their bills into the water.

Behind Albert, the stranger crouched low in the grass. With both hands, he grabbed a leather strap that ran diagonally from his right shoulder to his left hip, and pulled it over his head. The leather now dangled loosely into the grasses below his knees, for this was of no concern to him; it was only a means of carrying something precious on his back. He now turned this instrument around so that its thin, rigid arc of wood faced forward, toward Albert and the flock of geese. A taut thin line of string ran down its back. The stranger pulled an arrow from a long, narrow pouch. He placed it against the bow with the gentleness and deliberate care of someone playing a harp.

He raised his bow up to his shoulder and paused for a moment, just about the length of one long, slow breath. He slowly pulled the arrow back and the string moved with it. Then with a quick snapping motion, he pulled his thumb off the arrow. It shot forward.

Behind him, Albert heard a whirring noise and turned. But the arrow was not intended for him. It flew straight into a fat goose drinking at the water's edge.

The flock burst upward. Wings beat in panicked bursts. The cacophony of their barking made Albert's ears ring. He ran straight for the dead goose, the stranger behind him. Albert saw the heavy bird sink into the shallow water. Although he disliked the feel of water on his fur, hunger overrode his distaste. He plunged straight in, lowered his head, and closed his jaws around the limp neck. It moved like a rag. He struggled toward the muddy shore, dragging his dinner out of the water. He moved slowly, for the goose was heavy, nearly thrice his weight.

Whamp! Pain shot through Albert's right flank. The goose's neck fell out of his mouth and plunked down into the water. He turned and looked up. A tall, thin, strange-looking creature was running toward him. He had seen nothing like it in the forest. It ran straight up on its hind legs and waved its front legs about, yelling wildly. Albert's fur stood up. His back arched stiffly. He bared his teeth at the stranger and hissed. He hissed so hard that a rumbling formed way down in his throat.

But the stranger was not afraid of him. He bent down, put his front legs in the water, and gathered something up. Then he lobbed stone after stone at Albert, yelling and cursing until he lost his breath. Albert finally whimpered and slunk away, but not very far. He stayed close enough to watch. As the strange creature bent down and pulled the goose out of the water, Albert noticed that the fur on his head was the color of the midday sun.

The stranger's hair sparkled as he bent over the water. He picked up the goose by its feet and walked slowly out of the marsh. Mud sucked at his boots. But even when he reached dry land, the hunter still moved slowly, for the goose was heavy.

Albert crouched low in the marsh and began silently threading his way through the cattails. All urgency was gone now from the hunter's movements. A wide, flat meadow separated the marsh from the forest. The hunter crossed it slowly, his bow and his pouch of arrows slung across his back, one hand gripping the goose's feet as its long neck and head bobbed and swung loosely about, brushing against the meadow's tall grasses. The hunter was heading back the same way he had come — north, toward the plume of smoke on the other side of the forest.

The man's shoulders stooped slightly. When he neared the trees, he stopped and shifted the goose to his other hand. The goose would only get heavier. Sooner or later, the hunter would have to set down his prize and rest. Albert used every hunting skill he had acquired that summer as he shadowed the stranger.

He was silent but swift as he crossed the meadow and even followed the man down the middle of the path he took through through the forest, for the soft dirt and needles afforded Albert more silent passage than the thick carpet of dried, brittle leaves bordering the path. To some, Albert's eschewing the thick underbrush for the open path might seem reckless and foolhardy. But Albert knew silence was his best camouflage. And if there is anything a successful hunter knows, it is when to be cautious and when to be bold.

The hunter walked for a long time as Albert followed. The weak autumn sun rose higher, its light shifting as the forest changed. One moment, broad, wide shafts of sunlight would break through the trees and fan out until they reached the floor of the forest. A few steps later, nothing but dappled light penetrated the crowns of the trees, brightening up yellow leaves and making red ones blaze high overhead while Albert and the hunter walked underneath in deep shadows. But Albert and the hunter paid no mind to the sunlight and its antics with autumn colors.

Heaven had been the kind of place where Albert could bask in the sunlight or play hide-and-go-seek with it when it disappeared behind a cloud. But heaven was in the business of bliss. And this strange new place where Albert had recently landed was in the business of survival.

As the hunter walked, Albert heard the river. In some places, where the trees were particularly thin, the river grew louder. He was drawn to its chorus and wanted badly to go to the water's edge and drink. But Albert could not take his eyes off the man.

Albert did not feel that the man had stolen his goose. There was no sense that the goose was rightfully his. He had not yet learned to mark his territory; so he did not feel that the man was invading it. There was only one thing Albert felt; it was neither a sense of possession nor anger. Albert felt hunger. He was hollow inside. And he did not know if more geese would follow. He knew only that it was becoming colder and food was more scarce. So Albert did not let the hunter and his goose out of his sight.

The hunter pushed onward as the sun slowly slipped lower. The sound of the river receded. Albert pushed on. The trees were growing thinner. Albert saw trees that looked strange to him. Branches had been cut off at clean angles; clearly something other than the wind had done it. The smell of smoke grew stronger.

Albert did not particularly like the smell. But the hunter moved toward the smoke. Albert followed.

Eventually they reached a clearing. A cottage stood in the middle of it. Its walls were made of field stones, their uneven shapes and rough sides fit slowly and painstakingly together like the pieces of a jigsaw puzzle. A thatched roof covered the cottage. One wall was dominated by a massive stone chimney. The door stood in the middle of the opposite wall. And the two side walls each had one window, with no screens and no glass — only large square openings with wooden shutters. The shutters stood open. Smoke rose steadily from the chimney and curled in wisps against the gray-blue autumn sky.

As the hunter stepped into the clearing, the cottage door flew open. "Gregor!" a woman called out, her apron and long, full skirts billowing as she hurried toward them. Albert slipped off the path and into the underbrush as unobtrusively as a breath of air.

"Margrethe, I have brought you a goose."

Albert's haunches stood out as he studied the hunter's hand — waiting for him to drop the goose or lay it down, if only for an instant. But he never did. The hunter and the woman went inside. The man never let go of his prize. Albert had never gotten his chance.

He stayed low in the thicket and studied the clearing. There was only a well and one other building, a hut slightly smaller than the cottage with the same stone walls and thatched roof, but no chimney, no windows or shutters, and no steps — just one simple roughly hewn wooden door. Albert did not know what it was. These were the first people and the first buildings he had ever seen.

Albert explored the clearing from the safe vantage point of the underbrush and trees surrounding it. The clearing was an imperfect circle. He paced slowly around its perimeter. His only stroke of good fortune was his discovery of a puddle of rainwater. He crouched down and drank slowly, his ears rotated slightly outward, every sense attuned to the merest hint of human sound — an opening door, a footstep. But Albert heard nothing. He decided to rest and selected a spot with a direct view of the door. He laid down on his side, but his head remained erect and his eyes alert. He watched the cottage.

He heard kitchen sounds and chatter while the man and the woman busied themselves on the other side of the door. Presently, the whole clearing smelled of roasting goose. Albert's mouth watered. His tongue hung out. And his sides ached with hunger.

Soon the door opened. The hunter walked across the clearing and disappeared behind the hut. Albert seized his chance. He bolted across the clearing and shot into the cottage, his nose guiding him toward the roasting goose. But the moment he was inside, Albert shrunk back. He had never seen fire before. The goose was on a spit, suspended low over the flames.

He could not have gotten at it anyway. The woman was tending the fire and the meat, first stoking the flames, then basting the goose with a long-handled brush.

Fortunately, her back was turned to him. The goose's head and neck had been chopped cleanly off and lay discarded on a butcher block behind her. There was little meat on it, but it would have to do. Albert leapt up to the countertop. He crouched over the goose's head and closed his jaws around its neck for the second time that day.

Something crashed in the doorway behind him.

"Vile beast!"

Albert sprung from the countertop to the window sill and out into the clearing as the periphery of his vision caught a golden flash. Sunlight poured through the open cottage door as the hunter rushed through it, logs scattering at his feet.

The hunter grabbed his bow and pouch of arrows and vaulted through the open window. But Albert was faster. By the time the man was in the clearing, Albert had safely concealed himself in the underbrush, his jaws still gripped tightly around the goose's scrawny neck.

The man walked slowly around the clearing, bow and arrow in his hands. Sunlight flashed off his golden hair. As Albert watched, the shadows lengthened. The man eventually stopped pacing and took up a sentry position on the threshold of his cottage. The woman joined him.

"Margrethe, that is the creature that nearly stole our goose. I should have shot him in the marsh today. But I did not want to waste an arrow on something so lean."

"Ah, indeed, Gregor, there is no meat on those bones. But he is very clever."

"Did you see those eyes? Margrethe, there is something inside that creature. It is not entirely of this world."

Even though months had passed since Albert's fall from heaven, a bit of magic still clung stubbornly to him like cobwebs on a cat's whiskers. The hunter could see it, and it repelled him. Gregor believed he could see into an animal's soul. When he had looked into Albert's eyes, he saw an animal that was clever but duplicitous. Gregor saw an adversary, not an ally.

That would have to change, for Albert's sake, before winter settled in. He hunkered down in the brush to gnaw ravenously on the goose's neck as a thin sliver of moon rose and evening shadows swallowed the clearing. Soon the forest was dark and the clearing nearly so, except for slits of light breaking through the slats in the shutters — as bright and mysterious as a cat's eyes.

Albert waited until the fire was extinguished and the hunter and his wife went to bed. He heard them snoring before he dared creep out of the brush. He hurried across the clearing toward the stone chimney and hunkered down for the night, huddling against its warm stones as he drifted off to sleep. He pressed his side against the chimney. Tonight was noticeably colder than the night before.

He slept fitfully, napping rather than sleeping. He was awakened early by a light rustling of leaves. The light was a sludgy gray; it was the very first daylight of what would be a sluggish dawn. Albert raised his head. His ears twitched as he followed the noise. A blur sped across the clearing between the cottage and the shed. Albert fell on it, knowing with instinct it was a mouse, the same animal he had hunted on the forest floor. His jaws closed around its neck with lightning speed and snapped it. He dragged it into the underbrush and feasted. It was plump. Like those he had hunted in the summer.

Soon he saw more activity and knew the shed had something in it that was attracting mice. There were far too many coming and going, and they were all plump. Albert lay in the thicket and watched. He had chosen a vantage point from which he could eye both the door of the shed and the cottage. He was no longer interested in stealing roasted goose. It was too dangerous. But he had to keep an eye on the hunter and his wife. The cottage door soon opened, and the woman emerged, crossing the clearing toward the shed. When she opened the door, she screamed, "Gregor!"

The man bolted across the clearing.

"Mice! They are eating the grain! Look! We will have no bread this winter if this goes on. What will we do?"

Throughout the day, Albert rested in the thicket, watching and listening intently. The man spent a great deal of time tinkering with tools and wires and springy things. He put something inside the shed that night before he closed the door.

Albert became restless — and more alert — as nighttime encroached first upon the forest, then the clearing, and finally the cottage, extinguishing its fire. Albert listened. The man and the woman had settled in for the night.

Then Albert went to work. He approached the shed. A blur shot past him and sped under the door. Something snapped on the other side. Albert tried to get in, but he couldn't. He reached blindly under the door with one long, thin paw and batted about. He heard mice scurrying, but they remained just outside his reach.

He paced back and forth outside the shed. He smelled the mice. Finally, he withdrew to the warmth of the chimney, hungry and frustrated. He huddled, pushing every fiber of himself against the warm stones. The ground was colder tonight. The warmth of the chimney stones dissipated more quickly than the night before.

Albert barely closed his eyes. He waited for the first smidgeon of dawn and positioned himself against one wall of the hut, hidden from the cottage's view, but ready for the moment the man or woman opened the door.

Dawn came all too slowly. The man soon opened the cottage door and went to the shed immediately. Grain was as important to them as mice were to him, Albert could see that. As the man opened the door, Albert slunk along the shed's outer wall and slipped in behind him. Albert's eyes took in the sight of bushels and bales of grain, stacked floor to ceiling. But his eyes also feasted upon the sight of mice, scores of mice, burrowed everywhere. As Albert watched, he understood that the man could not see the mice; he could not see much at all inside the dimly lit shed.

The man bent over his trap. A dead mouse was in it, its neck broken so cleanly and swiftly it would have done justice to a cat. Albert admired the man's work, but he had felled only one. The woman understood this too.

"How many do you suppose there are, Gregor?"

"I do not know Margrethe. I will have to make more traps."

Throughout the day, the man worked. Albert watched and devised a plan.

Albert spent the whole day in the shed, remaining inside when the door was closed that night. By nightfall, the man had placed six traps throughout the shed. Fortunately, Albert could see in the dark. He knew where the traps lay. Still, he hunkered down and waited until he heard one after the other and all six had snapped.

Then Albert went to work. It was child's play, catching mice inside the granary. Even if they fled from him and shot out under the door into the clearing, the smell of grain always lured them back. As the first light of dawn slipped under the door, Albert was dispatching his seventh mouse. He had eaten one early in the evening, but saved six. He hid all six and concealed himself far back in the deep shadows of the granary.

As the man and the woman opened the door, sunlight filtered in. They took long sticks and slid their traps out into the clearing. All were full.

Now it was Albert's turn. He would have to do something more bold than he had ever done before. His instincts were to avoid the humans. But winter was approaching. Albert felt it seeping into his bones. And he was hunting not just for food, but also for a warm hearth.

So Albert bent over a dead mouse, seizing its limp neck between his jaws and walked out into the clearing. He walked right up to the hunter and dropped it at his feet. He slipped back into the granary and retrieved another, dropping his second trophy at the woman's feet. Back and forth Albert went, swiftly and silently, not pausing to look at the humans until he had methodically delivered his six presents — three for the man and three for the woman.

Then Albert walked twenty paces across the clearing and sat down in his most dignified pose. He looked at the humans for the first time since depositing the mice at their feet. Both were staring at him silently, their mouths open in astonishment. But Albert did not stare back. He turned his head slightly and looked at them from an oblique angle as a gesture of feline respect. He slowly slid both eyelids halfway closed in a sort of soft wink.

Albert then commenced grooming himself, first by delicately licking one paw and rubbing his face and ears. With meticulous care, he repeated the entire procedure with the opposite paw. Albert's gamble paid off. The hunter did not rush into the cottage for his bow and arrow — or his axe. He did not curse. He stood silently in the clearing, looking down at Albert and the half-dozen gifts arranged neatly at his feet.

The hunter understood that he was in the presence of a fellow hunter — one whose skill matched his own. The hunter felt something new toward Albert. He felt respect.

On that day, Albert was immediately allowed full run of the granary. By late autumn, he was allowed just inside the cottage. However, it was clearly understood by all that he was not to jump up on the table and help himself to dinner. But this injunction was of little import, because juicy scraps somehow always found their way to the floor. As winter encroached upon the clearing, the hunter and his wife were allowing Albert to inch closer and closer toward the warmth of their hearth. Before spring arrived, Albert had also secured for himself a place in their hearts.

THE END

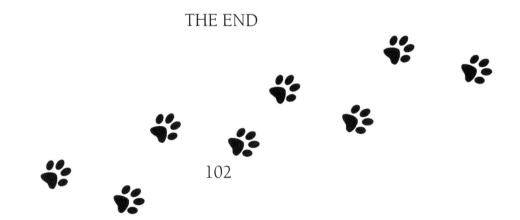

About the Author

Janet Rhodes has honed her fiction-writing skills by attending numerous classes, workshops, writers' groups, and conferences, including the UC Berkeley extension and Squaw Valley Community of Writers. She is also the author of Chocolate and Cabernet, which is available at Amazon.com/CreateSpace: http://www.createspace.com/3388474
  Several of her articles have been published in San Francisco Bay Area publications.
janet@bratcat.com

About the Illustrator
Michael Rhodes took apart grocery bags at the age of five to create pads of drawing paper. Decades later, he has still not stopped, although he has switched from grocery bags and crayons to charcoal, paint, pen and ink, and computer. He has taught web design at Silicon Valley College, and has taught cartooning classes to elementary school children. His cartoons may be viewed at crtoons.com
  mike@crtoons.com

Mike and Janet are the co-owners of BratCat Productions, which provides writing, editing, and design services. For a complete list of books and comics, please visit **www.bratcat.com**